For Elaine, Joan, the Leigh Writers,
and for Marion without whom...
C.F.

To my Grandads
S.J.

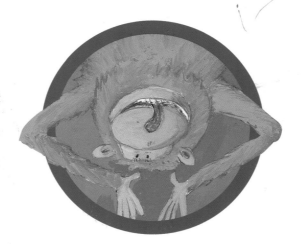

Ω
Published by
PEACHTREE PUBLISHERS, LTD.
1700 Chattahoochee Avenue
Atlanta, Georgia 30318-2112

www.peachtree-online.com

First published in Great Britain in 2001 by Orchard Books

Printed in Hong Kong/China

10 9 8 7 6 5 4 3 2 1
First Edition

ISBN: 1-56145-251-3

Cataloging-in-Publication Data is available from the Library of Congress

Where's Your Smile, Crocodile?

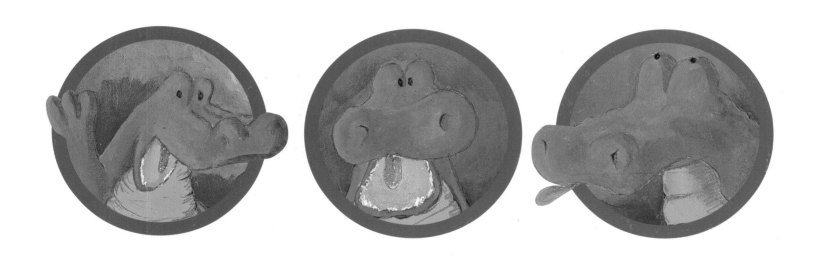

by Claire Freedman
illustrated by Sean Julian

Ω
PEACHTREE
ATLANTA

One morning Kyle the Crocodile
woke up feeling very grumpy.
"Looks like you've lost your smile, Kyle,"
said his mom. "Why don't you go out and play?
You'll soon find it again."

So off Kyle trudged, through the tangled jungle to Parrot's tree.

"Oh dear," Parrot squawked. "Where's your smile, Crocodile?"

"I've lost it," said Kyle.

"Never mind," replied Parrot. "I'll cheer you up with some of my silly noises. You'll soon find it again."

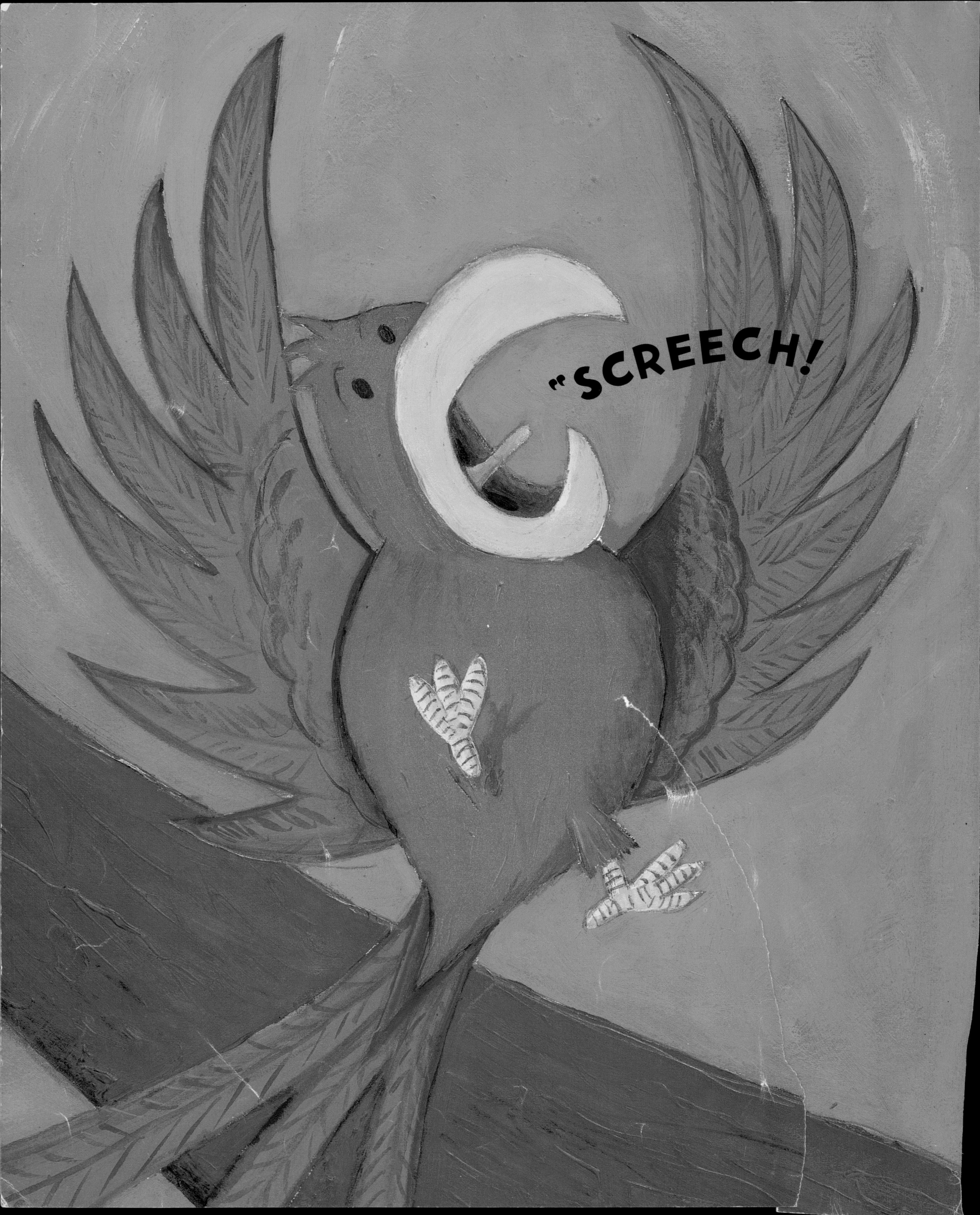
"SCREECH!

"SQUAWK! SCREECH!" went Parrot as he whizzed round and round on his branch. All the animals who saw laughed and laughed. **Ha ha ha!**

But Kyle didn't laugh. "My smile's not here," he said. "It must be somewhere else." And away he crawled to look for it.

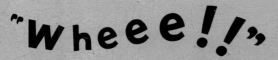**"Wheee!!"**
Suddenly down swung Orange Monkey.
"Oh dear, oh dear," he chattered.
"Where's your smile, Crocodile?"

"I've lost it," replied Kyle.
"Never mind," said Orange Monkey.
"You'll soon find it again. Why don't I cheer
you up with some of my funny faces?"

"**YAHOO!** **YAHOO!** **YAHOO!**" Orange Monkey made her angry face. . .

and her CrAZY face. . .

and her very funny hanging-upside-down-from-a-tree face.

All the animals who saw laughed and laughed. **Hee hee hee!**

But Kyle didn't laugh. "My smile's not here," he said. "It must be somewhere else."
And off he clomped down to the riverbank to find it.

"Oh dear," Elephant trumpeted.
"Where's your smile, Crocodile?"
"I've lost it," sighed Kyle.

"Never mind," said Elephant. "You'll soon
find it again. Watch me—I'll cheer you up."

Elephant blew big noisy bubbles in the water and squirted it everywhere. All the animals who saw laughed and laughed.

Ha ha ha!
Hee hee hee!

But Kyle didn't laugh.
"My smile's not here," he said.
"It must be somewhere else."
And away he plodded through the jungle creepers and lotus blossoms. . .

. . .where he found Little Lion Cub
sitting all by himself on an old termite hill.
   "Oh dear," said Kyle. "Whatever is the matter?"
   "I've lost my way home!" Little Lion Cub sniffed.
   "And I've lost my smile," said Kyle.
"Shall we look for them together?"

So side by side they searched
through the jungle.

To cheer up Little Lion Cub,
Kyle made some of Parrot's silly noises.

"SCREECH!
SQUAWK! SCREECH!"

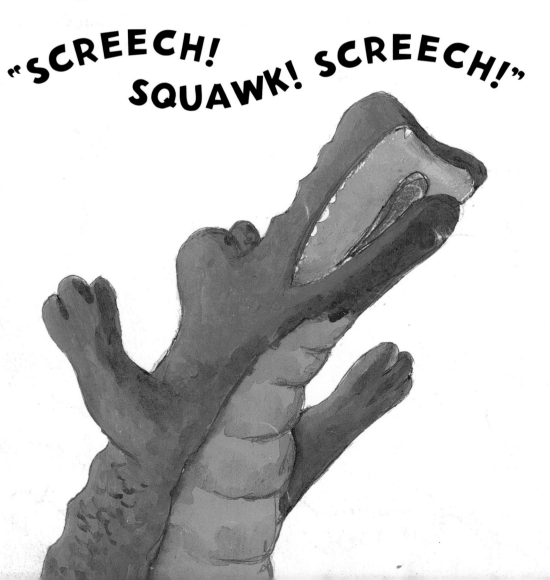

He made some funny
faces like Orange Monkey.

"YAHOO! YAHOO! YAHOO!"

And he blew big noisy bubbles in the water, like Elephant.

"BURBLE! BURBLE! BURBLE!"

Little Lion Cub soon felt happier.

When they reached the deep purple caves,
Little Lion Cub suddenly squealed.
　"This is where I live! Thank you.
I've found the way home again."
　"I'm glad I could help," said Kyle.
　"And guess what?" said Little Lion Cub.

...ve found your smile, Kyle."

..ve I?" said Kyle. "Where is it then?"

..ack on your face,"

..ghed Little Lion Cub,

..where it belongs!"

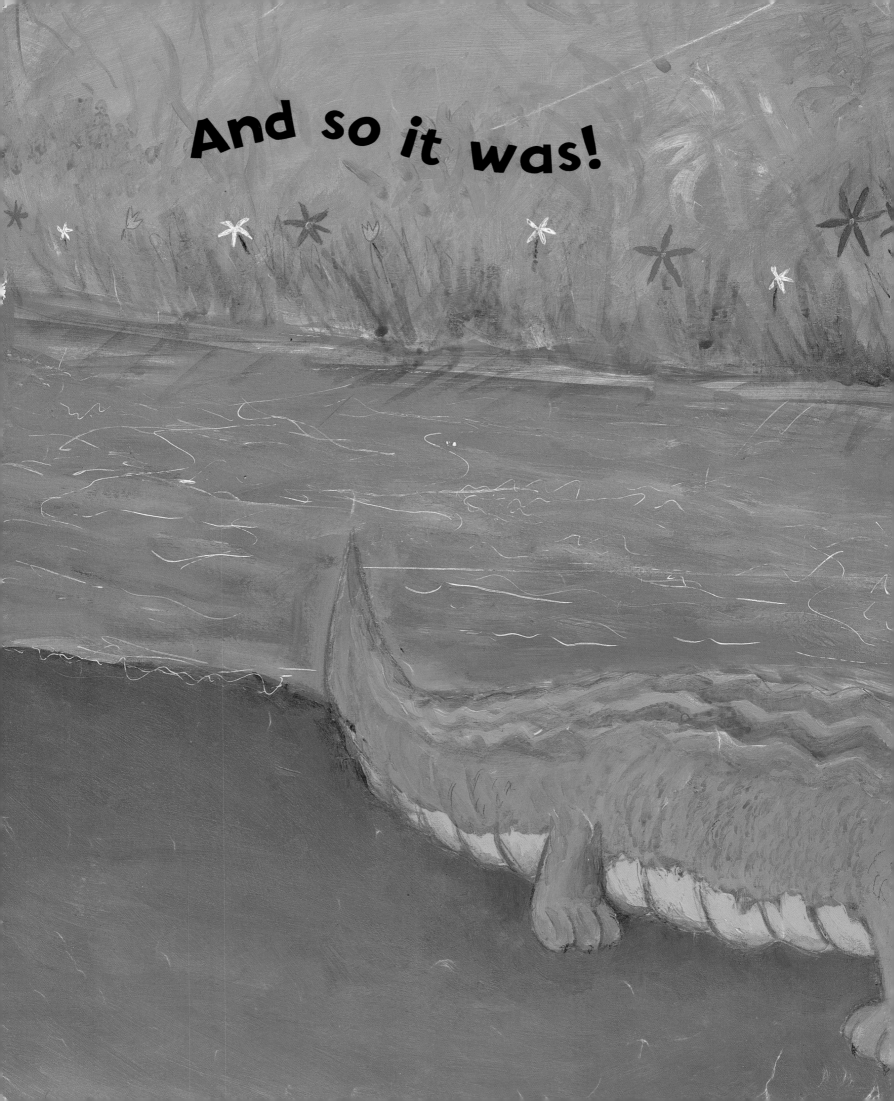

And so it was!